W9-BLP-739

As the Roadrunner Runs

A FIRST BOOK OF MAPS

by Gail Hartman

illustrated by Cathy Bobak

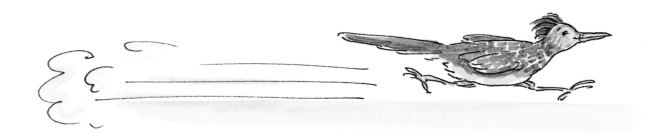

Bradbury Press · New York

Maxwell Macmillan Canada   Toronto
Maxwell Macmillan International
New York   Oxford   Singapore   Sydney

Bradbury Press
Macmillan Publishing Company
866 Third Avenue
New York, NY 10022

Maxwell Macmillan Canada, Inc.
1200 Eglinton Avenue East
Suite 200
Don Mills, Ontario M3C 3N1

Macmillan Publishing Company is part of the Maxwell Communication
Group of Companies.
First edition
Printed in Singapore by Toppan Printing Company on recycled paper
10   9   8   7   6   5   4   3   2   1

Library of Congress Cataloging-in-Publication Data
Hartman, Gail.
As the roadrunner runs : a first book of maps / by Gail Hartman ;
illustrated by Cathy Bobak.—1st ed.
p.   cm.
Summary: Simple maps show how different animals, including a
lizard, a jackrabbit, a roadrunner, mules, and deer, travel through
an area of the Southwest.
ISBN 0-02-743092-8
[1. Geography—Fiction.   2. Southwest, New—Fiction.   3. Animals—
Fiction.   4. Maps—Fiction.]   I. Bobak, Cathy, ill.   II. Title.
PZ7.H26733Au   1994
[E]—dc20   94-13

For my dad
　—*G.H.*

For my grandmothers
　—*C.B.*

In the desert a path winds
between two saguaro cactuses,

past a barrel cactus,

to a red rock boulder baking in the sun.

saguaro cactus

barrel cactus

red rock boulder

THE LIZARD'S MAP

Past the railroad station,

past the old well,

is a place where tasty grass grows.

railroad station

old well

tasty grass

THE JACKRABBIT'S MAP

The road crosses the railroad track

and passes the store

on the way to the cabin,
where the whirligig stands.

railroad tracks

store

cabin

whirligig

THE ROADRUNNER'S MAP

A sign marks a trail

that passes tall rocks

and leads to a lookout high
above the canyon floor.

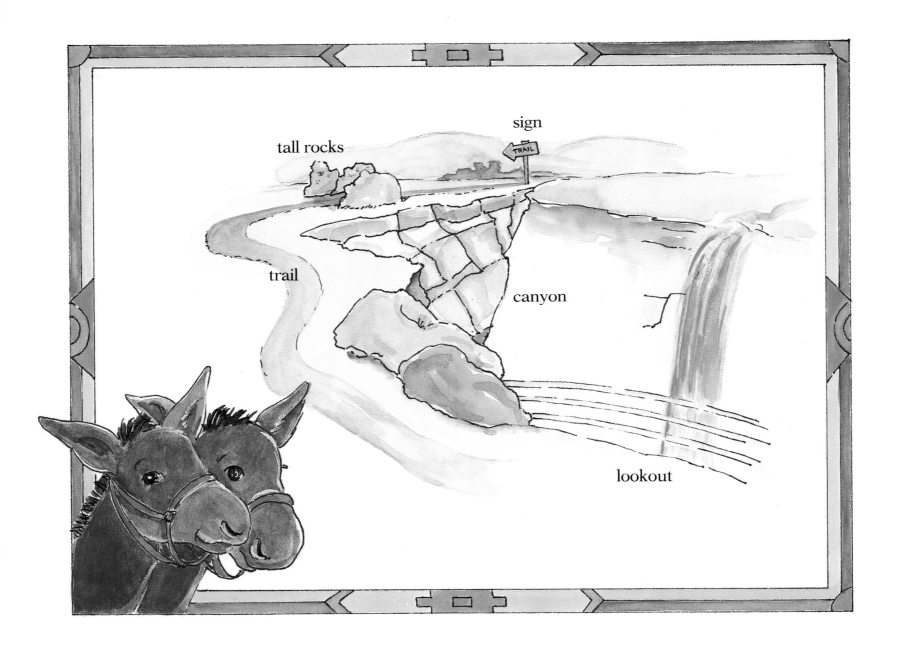

THE MULES' MAP

On the far side of the canyon,

through a grove of aspen trees,

across a grassy meadow,
there is a stream of cool, clear water.

aspen grove

stream

meadow

THE DEER'S MAP

When the wind blows,
it whispers in the leaves on quaking aspens

and whistles across the canyon.

It stops to play with a whirligig

and tease a window curtain.

Then it rushes past the train station

to cool a red rock boulder.

aspen grove

stream

meadow

sign

canyon

railroad tracks

lookout

trail

tall rocks

store

cabin

whirligig

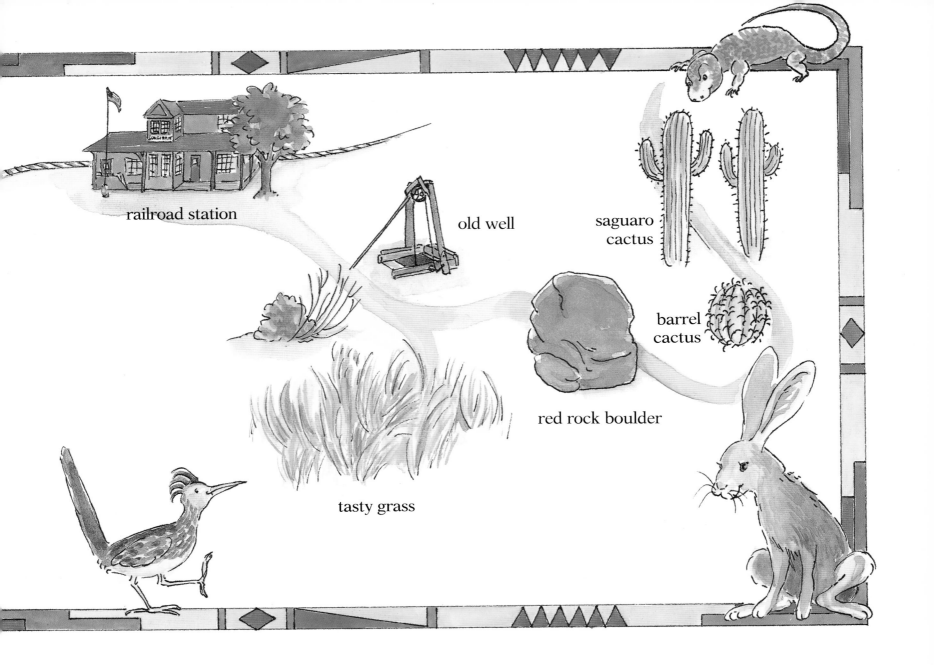

railroad station

old well

saguaro cactus

barrel cactus

red rock boulder

tasty grass

THE BIG MAP